Molly's friend Jane has come to play.
Tom the cat is a little jealous.

Tom wants to play, too.

I wonder if they'll let me join in?
thinks Tom.

"I know how to hold baby dolls,"
says Tom.

But Molly and Jane won't let Tom play.
"There are only two dolls," they say.

Tom is so angry, he does something silly.
He knocks over a potted plant.

"Who made this mess?" asks Mother.

Tom, who by now is feeling sorry, hides behind the chest.

Molly thinks, I wasn't very nice to Tom . . .

So she takes the blame for him
and goes to stand in the corner.

Tom is really sorry now.
Jane has gone and Molly is sad.

"I still love you, Tom," says Molly.
"And it **is** fun to play, just the two of us!"